Play It Again

by Regina Kyle

Play It Again

Copyright © 2020 by Regina Kyle

Cover art by Mayhem Creations
Edited by Jane Haertel

www.ReginaKyle.com

Give feedback on the book at:
reginakyleauthor@gmail.com

Facebook: ReginaKyleAuthor

First Edition

Printed in the U.S.A

Dedication

For the real David and Chris. My friends. My neighbors. My inspiration. I wrote your story. You're stuck with me now.

-Chapter One-

David

I thought I was prepared to see him again. But the minute Chris walks into the bar, my pulse kicks into overdrive and the hair on my arms and at the nape of my neck springs to attention. He's the only guy I've ever loved, and he's here. Our eyes lock when he spots me, and then he's crossing toward me, my heart hammering with every step he takes.

My fingers stumble on the keyboard of the Steinway baby grand I play every Thursday through Sunday from nine to midnight. It's not Carnegie Hall, but it pays the bills, at least until something better, like a gig with an orchestra or in a Broadway pit, lands in my lap. Fortunately, most of the patrons are too deep in conversation—or too drunk—to notice my slipup, and I segue seemingly effortlessly into the opening bars of "As Time Goes By."

"My favorite." Chris leans against the piano, a hesitant smile briefly lifting the corners of his mouth, and signals for a waitress. "You remembered."

I did, but I'm not about to admit that to him. This time I'm keeping my emotions under lock and key. Like Fort Knox.

"People love it. It's good for tips."

As if on cue, a pretty, perky twenty-something—probably a coed from one of the nearby colleges—smiles at me and drops a five into the large brandy snifter I use as a tip jar. I nod my thanks and she goes back to her friends, leaving me free to study Chris as he orders his drink.

My fingers almost stumble again. Damn him for looking even better than he did in our conservatory days. Same intense, enigmatic hazel eyes, more green today than brown. Same aquiline nose. Same strong, square jaw, dotted with sexy, late-night stubble. But now the whole package reads more hot businessman than dancer-in-training. Although I'd bet my Yamaha DGX-660 portable keyboard that beneath his designer duds he's got the same buff ballet body he did back in school. He'd have to, as a principal dancer for the prestigious San Francisco Ballet.

Maybe it's the clothes—pale gray, slim-fit button-down shirt, tight, dark jeans, suede oxfords in a soft charcoal—that make this man. Or it could be the glasses. Dark Harry Potter rims that give him an air of maturity.

Then there's the hair. It's a little longer than I remember, chestnut strands curling over his collar. I wonder briefly if his wife prefers it that way, then swallow the hard, bilious knot of jealousy that rises in my throat. What right do I have to be jealous? Chris made his choice five years ago. One kiss was all it had taken for me to know how good it could be with us. And for him to run as fast as his feet would take him in the other direction.

His drink comes—an old-fashioned, another thing that's changed since college, when we downed wine coolers like they were water. The choice of cocktail is like a punch in my gut. It's the consummate man's man's drink. Practically screams, "Sorry, dude. I'm still straight."

"Any requests?" I ask, determined not to let him see how rattled he's got me.

"Can you take a break? I'd really like to talk. It's important."

It must be—or he must think it is—for him to come all this way after all this time to see me. Still, I shake my head. "Can't. I just got on half an hour ago."

"I can wait." He takes a sip of his drink then sets it down on a cocktail napkin. Not on the bare wood of the piano, like I warned him against at the conservatory more times than I can count. My stupid heart flip-flops. He may have wanted to erase me from his life, but he hasn't forgotten everything.

"It might be a while before I can get free," I say, mentally crossing my fingers at the white lie. My sets are only about an hour long, and I usually take a ten-minute break between them.

"I'm in no rush." He runs a finger along the edge of his glass, then touches it to his lips. The unconsciously sexy gesture makes my damn disobedient dick twitch, and I say a silent prayer of thanks that it's hidden under the Steinway.

The final chords of "As Time Goes By" echo around us as my brain searches for another song. I don't usually have this much trouble figuring out what to play next. My repertoire is pretty extensive. Plus, I keep an iPad with my favorite sheet music app handy for any songs I don't know by memory.

But I'm finding it more than a little bit distracting having the love of my life standing not three feet from me, his mesmerizing hazel eyes tracking my every move.

He gives me a smile that's incongruously both confident and nervous. "Of all the gin joints, in all the towns, in all the world, I walk into yours."

I shake my head and start in on "Fly Me To The Moon." Can't go wrong with Sinatra. It's always a crowd favorite. "Except you're no Ilsa, and I'm no Rick. You knew I'd be here. And I knew you were coming."

Thanks to the cryptic Facebook message he sent me last week. What I don't know is why he's here. What does he want, after all this time?

It's a question I'm too chickenshit to ask. So instead I decide to go for the cheap shot. It won't be my finest moment, but I tell myself it's his fault for showing up practically out of the blue, after five years of radio silence.

"How's your wife?" The last word comes out like a curse, leaving a sour taste in my mouth.

A shadow crosses Chris's handsome face, and I immediately regret the low blow. "We split up. Almost a year ago. The divorce was final in March."

Holy shit. He and Sonja are splitsville?

My mouth goes dry and my heart free falls to my stomach. It's official. I'm the biggest douchecanoe on the planet.

"I'm sorry." It's not a lie. I am. I don't wish divorce on anyone. Even the guy who's the source of the biggest heartache of my 27-year-old life. And the girl he chose over me.

But I'd be lying if I didn't admit that a small part of me is also curious as fuck. Why did they break up? Was that the reason for his visit?

Chris takes another sip of his old-fashioned. "Truth is, it was over a long time ago, but neither one of us wanted to be the one to pull the plug."

So what changed? I want to scream. But a middle-aged man who's clearly had too much to drink stumbles over and asks me to play "Piano Man"—a request I must get ten times a night, minimum—putting our conversation on pause. I spend way too long promising him— repeatedly—that I'll get to it in the next set. Finally, his booze-soaked brain seems to understand what I'm saying and he shuffles off, humming the harmonica part.

As he goes, Chris's eyes catch mine for a brief, heart-stopping moment. Then he glances toward the door that leads to the restrooms and office.

"I was hoping we could talk somewhere more private."

Exactly what I'm afraid of. I don't trust myself to be alone with him. Which is why I suggested we meet here, at my very public workplace.

"Please."

His simple, one-word plea wrecks me. I'm no more able to resist him now than I was five years ago.

I close my eyes, needing to erect some sort of barrier between us, and let muscle memory take over, guiding my fingers over the keys. "After this song."

Time seems to stretch as I pound out the last chorus. When I'm done, I lean into the mic and announce that I'll be taking a break. Yeah, it's early. But my boss will just have to deal with it. If he bitches, I'll offer to play an extra set.

I pocket my tips from the jar, leaving a few bills so it doesn't look depressingly desolate, and stand. Chris tosses back the rest of his drink and follows suit. Wordlessly, I lead him through the door, down the hall past the restrooms and office, and into the alley behind the club.

The outside door closes behind us with an ominous click that echoes in the narrow passageway. Chris leans against the brick wall, pulls a pack of Newports from his back pocket, and slides out a cigarette.

"You still smoking?" I ask stupidly. Duh. Why else would he be carrying cigarettes around? It's not like he's a POW, trading them for food.

He puts the cigarette between his lips and stuffs the pack back in his pocket, trading it for a lighter. "Only when I'm nervous."

He's nervous? My heart is racing like I've run a goddamn marathon.

I pick a spot on the wall opposite him and rest my back on the rough, red-brown bricks. The fingers of my right hand tap a staccato rhythm on the soft cotton of my khakis. My nervous habit. "Why?"

He flicks the lighter, holds it up to the end of his cigarette, and inhales. The glow gives his face an eerie cast in the half-light of the alley. "Why what?"

"Why so nervous?"

He takes a long drag on his cigarette and, ever the gentleman, turns his head to blow a puff of smoke off to his left, away from me. "I've never done this before."

"Done what?"

My already pounding pulse kicks up a notch. This is it. The moment of truth. I'm finally going to find out what the hell he's doing here. In a seedy back alley. With me.

"Apologized to someone I hurt as much as I hurt you." Chris

tosses the cigarette to the ground and snuffs it out under the heel of his shoe. "I'm sorry I freaked out when you kissed me. You were my friend—my best friend—and I acted like a complete asshole, shutting you out. Waiting this long to try to make things right. My only excuse is—I have no excuse. I guess I'm just not as brave as you are."

"Me?" I make an unattractive sound that's somewhere between a laugh and a snort. "Brave?"

"You're brave enough to be your true, authentic self. That's more than I can say for me. But I'd like the chance to change that."

"How?"

He scrubs an unsteady hand through his slightly too-long hair. "By asking you out. On a date."

It's a good thing the brick wall is supporting me, otherwise I'd be on the asphalt with Chris's cigarette butt. "You want to go on a date? With me? Now?"

"Better late than never, right?" he says with a nervous chuckle.

"Is it?" My heart screams *fuck, yeah*. But my head—the one on my shoulders, not below my belt—isn't such an easy mark. It's telling me to slow things down. Protect myself.

"It can be." He shoves his hands into the pockets of his jeans.

"How do you know I'm not with someone?" I ask, even though I'm totally not.

He blushes, and it's so fucking adorable I almost say yes to the date right then and there. "I've been stalking you on Facebook. And Instagram. No pics of you with anyone. And your relationship status is single."

"So you're what?" I ask. "Gay? Bi? Pan?"

"I'm gay."

"And you're out? Is that why you and Sonja called it quits?"

He stares at the tips of his shoes. "Not exactly."

I slam my palms against the wall so hard they sting, pain radiating up my arms. Stupid move for a guy who makes his living with his hands. But that just goes to show how fucking frustrated I am. It's like we're back in college, when I was out and Chris was—confused. That confusion almost killed me. And I'm not about to subject myself to that a second time.

It's like my grandmother—God rest her loud and proud Italian soul—used to say. Fool me once, shame on you. Fool me twice, shame on me.

"I can't do this again."

I push off the unforgiving bricks and head for the door. I've got to get back inside ASAP, to the emotional safety of the crowded club. The longer I'm this close to him, his tangy, woodsy cologne filling my nostrils, overpowering the smells of the city, the more my resolve chips away.

And I need every damn bit of resolve I can muster.

But Chris has other ideas. He snags my arm as I pass, stopping me. The heat of his hand burns into my biceps, like he's branding me as his.

"Don't go." His voice is soft, almost a whisper. And desperate. "Let me explain."

It's the desperation that gets me. I've always been a sucker for a dude in distress.

"Explain away." I shrug off his hand and fold my arms across my chest. Listening is one thing. Touching is another.

"I'm out." He shifts his weight restlessly from one foot to the other, still somehow managing to imbue the restive movement with the easy grace of a dancer. "Mostly."

"What's mostly?"

"Sonja knows. A few close friends. Some of my family."

"Some?" I arch a brow at him, although I'm not sure he can read my facial expressions in the dimly lit alley.

"My sister. She's cool with it."

Which means his parents, who probably won't be quite so cool with their only son's sexual awakening as a gay man, are still in the dark. My lips are pressed together in a thin, exasperated line, but that doesn't stop a sigh from escaping. This is looking more and more like a bad rerun of our senior year.

"Let me ask you something." He nods, as if I'm waiting for his permission to continue. Spoiler alert: I'm not. "You're a good-looking guy. I assume you've dated your share of dudes. Gone out in public. Held hands walking down the street. Made out in the back row at the movies."

Maybe even fucked—or been fucked by—a guy or two or ten. But I'm not going there, for reasons I don't want to examine too closely. It's not like I've been celibate, although I can count my lovers on one hand. No one's ever measured up to Chris, and as hard as I've tried, I've never really gotten over him. Still, I've got no right to expect him to live like a monk.

He ducks his head and his hair flops over his eyes, shielding his face. "No."

"No to what?"

"To all of it."

The shock of his answer rolls through me, making me

stumble. I mean, just look at him. He's like a Greek god, only better. He could have any guy he wanted. And yet, he hasn't.

"Then how do you know—?"

His head snaps up.

"How do I know I'm gay?" he finishes for me. "Trust me, I know. I don't need to fuck a bunch of randoms to figure out that I prefer dudes."

"Who said anything about fucking?" Sure, I'd thought it. But I didn't say it. Has he added mind reader to his list of talents postcollege? "I'm talking about dating."

"I've got nothing against dating." Chris shuffles his feet again and starts, then stops, to reach for the pack of cigarettes in his back pocket. There's something he's not telling me.

"Then what's stopping you?" I press. It's taken five years for us to get to this point. I'm not letting him leave until I get some goddamn answers.

"There's only one guy I want to date."

Before I can fully process what he's telling me, his hand is on my chest, fisting the soft cotton of my shirt, pulling me in. Someone—I think it's me—lets out a soft oof as our bodies and mouths meet.

It's the polar opposite of the last—and only—time we kissed, when I took the lead. This time Chris is in control. He tastes like bourbon and bitters and citrus as he brushes his mouth over mine, slipping his tongue inside when my lips part to suck in a ragged breath.

I mimic his move, bunching his shirt in my fingers as the kiss goes on and on. His lips are firm. Greedy. Hypnotic. The longer the kiss goes, the deeper it gets. Our tongues join in on the action, then our hands, exploring, then our bodies, rocking against each other.

"Fuck." He moans into my mouth and rolls his hips, letting me feel every inch of his stiffening cock, as rock-hard as my own. "I knew it would be as good the second time."

His words plant a seed of self-doubt that takes root and spreads like wildfire. Is he really here because he wants me? Or am I just a safe choice for his first gay sexual experience?

I wrench my lips from his and shove at his chest. But that buff ballet body I suspected was lurking under his tailored shirt and tight jeans is immovable, and now I'm stuck with my palms pressed against a set of pecs that would rival Captain America's.

He drops his forehead to mine and lets out a long, low sigh that washes over me, ruffling my hair, teasing my earlobe, weakening my fragile defenses. "Shit. I'm sorry. I'm moving too fast. I know. But I want this so fucking bad."

"Want what?" I muster the nerve to ask, tipping my head back so I can look him in the eye when he answers. "Me, or—?"

I can't bring myself to finish the question, but he knows where I'm going, and from the scowl that darkens his handsome face, he's not too happy about it. "You think I'm here for a quick, easy lay? If that were all I wanted, I could have gotten it back in San Francisco. I didn't have to travel across the damn country."

He makes a good point, but I'm still not convinced. Years of second-guessing my impulsive decision to kiss my best friend have taken a toll on my self-confidence where Chris is concerned, and I tell him as much. "I'm just having a hard time believing that, after years of no contact, you suddenly discovered you couldn't live without me."

He lets his hands fall to his sides and steps back, giving me the space I need to sort out the jumble of emotions tossing and turning inside me.

"Look, I get why you don't trust me. If I was in your position, I wouldn't trust me, either. All I'm asking is that you give me a chance to be brave. Like you." He takes another step back and jams his hands in his pockets. "Meet me tomorrow night. Lincoln Center. I've got tickets to Giselle. The show starts at 8:00. I'll be waiting by the fountain."

Without another word, he turns on his heel and takes off down the alleyway, leaving me hard, horny, and totally off-balance.

-Chapter Two-

Chris

I've performed in front of thousands of people all over the world. Danced the Prince in Nureyev's *Sleeping Beauty* at the Palais Garnier. Even nailed the hauntingly beautiful—and extraordinarily difficult—pas de deux from the third act of Don Quixote at the White House. And not once—not even performing for the leader of the free world and his entire family—did I have stage fright. An adrenaline rush? Sure. But nothing even close to the sheer, unadulterated, almost crippling panic I feel now, standing next to the Revson Fountain in the middle of Josie Robertson Plaza in my teal, wool-blend Tom Ford suit, waiting for the guy I'm pretty sure I've loved since I was eighteen.

I check my watch for the hundredth time. Only fifteen minutes until curtain, and the crowd outside the Metropolitan Opera House is getting thinner by the second. If David doesn't show up soon, I'm going to have no choice but to go in without him.

Fuck. I'm an idiot. I can't even text him, since I was too busy making a big, dramatic exit to remember to ask for his cell number.

Goddamn drama queen.

But I can send him a Facebook message. If he hasn't blocked me after I practically mauled him yesterday. You'd think I never kissed a guy before. Which, of course, I haven't. Except for that one time. With him.

I pull out my phone and shoot him a quick—and I hope not too desperate-sounding—message. When I'm done, I close the app and glance at the time on the screen. Five more minutes have ticked by. Time to head inside.

Alone.

"Nice suit." David's voice makes my head snap up and my pulse stutter. "Made it easy to spot you."

An intoxicating mix of relief and euphoria floods my veins. *He's here*, my heart sings. *He came.*

"What can I say?" I tug at the cuff of my jacket, suddenly wishing I'd gone with my more traditional navy Hugo Boss. "I like to stand out in a crowd."

"You always did." He blushes. "Stand out, that is."

"Thanks. I think." I take a second to study him. He looks good, too, in a pair of pale blue linen pants and a simple, classic white button-down. He's tried to tame his normal mess of dark curls, and while the end result isn't entirely successful, I'm touched that he made the effort for me. At least, my foolish heart hopes it's for me, and not the ballet.

The ballet. My eyes dart to the main entrance of the theater, where the last few stragglers are rushing to get inside before the lights dim. "We should go in. The show's about to start."

"Sorry." He blushes again. I'd forgotten how easily he did that. And how fucking adorable it is. "The 1 train was running late."

"You're here now. That's all that matters."

"I almost wasn't," he admits as we start toward the theater.

"I changed my mind about a thousand times in the past twenty-four hours."

"So what was the deciding factor?" We're walking side by side, stride for stride, and my hand aches to reach for his. I shove it into my pocket instead, not because I'm afraid of guy-on-guy PDA but because I'm determined to take things slower than I did last night. To wait for David to make the next move, follow his cues. "My charm? My good looks?"

"Neither. It was something you said in the alley."

I hand over our tickets to a smiling older woman in a red vest and a "Live, Love, Ballet" pin who directs us to a staircase on our left and tells us to enjoy the show.

"What did I say?" I ask as we head up the stairs to the balcony.

"I guess it wasn't so much what you said, it was what you did. You took a risk. Came all the way here. Apologized. Asked me out. I figured the least I could do is give you the same consideration."

"Ask me out?" I tease, knowing that's not what he means. "Spoiler alert: my answer is yes."

He laughs, and it sends ripples of warmth through my body. I've always loved David's laugh. Easy. Hearty. Infectious. David's the guy you want in the audience at a comedy club, the one whose rich, booming laughter gets everyone else going.

But this laugh is different. It's softer and sweeter. More importantly, it tells me that, as nervous as he is about this date, he's starting to relax. And that's what I want. David to relax so we can get past this awkward are-we-or-aren't-we stage.

Because if I have any say in it, we are. We totally are.

"No, take a risk," he says, his eyes suddenly serious, their intensity a stark contrast to his laughter. "Give you a chance, like you said. It's only a date, right? We're not talking lifetime commitment. Hearts and flowers and all the crap."

"Right," I agree, mentally crossing my fingers behind my back for lying. Every relationship has to start somewhere, right? Or restart, given that ours began almost ten years ago. "Only a date."

"One date," David repeats, as if he's trying to convince himself of something. "How hard can that be?"

Oh, it can be hard. In fact, it's getting harder by the second.

I pull my mind out of the gutter and show our tickets to the usher, who points us to our seats. We're in a box on the far left, about twenty feet above the stage. Not the best view if sight lines are your primary concern. But if privacy is your objective—like it is for me—then these are the best seats in the house, off to the side and hidden from view by a heavy red velvet curtain.

"These are ours," I say, taking one seat and gesturing for David to sit in the other.

He sits down beside me just as the lights dim. There's no more talking for a while—as fellow artists, we know better than to commit that breach of theater etiquette—but about halfway through the first act, right at the point where Albrecht and Giselle do their pas de deux, I feel David's thigh brush against mine.

It's the slightest of touches, but it stops my breath in my throat. It's a good thing I know this ballet by heart because all my attention has shifted to the man next to me. The way his untamable hair spills into his gorgeous gray-green eyes. The sexy thump of his pulse at the hollow where his neck meets his collarbone. The rise and fall of his chest, in time with Adolphe Adam's music.

I don't know why I thought it would be a good idea to be confined in close quarters with him for almost three hours. Just the two of us. Alone. In the damn dark. I just wanted to be near him, our private box a bubble, insulating us from the rest of the world while we watched one of the most romantic ballets ever created. Kind of our own Pretty Woman moment.

But this? It's torture. Fucking torture. I don't know how Richard Gere managed to keep his hands off Julia Roberts in that box at *La Traviata*.

David's thigh brushes mine again, but this time it stays there. Heat burns through two layers of fabric. A second later, his hand is on mine, too, warm and solid and steadying, even as it makes my heart rate kick up a notch.

I'm hyper aware of him now. Giselle can go jump in a goddamn lake for all I care. The only thing that matters is David. That he's here. That he's touching me. That after all the years and all the miles between us, we've managed to get to this place, this point.

I can't erase those years. And I don't want to. They've shaped the man I am. Changed me. Matured me. I'm sure they've done the same for David. But the miles—that's something I'm hoping I can change.

Not that I'm sharing that with David. At least, not yet. I don't want to scare him off. He's thinking one date. He doesn't need to know my mind's skipped way the hell ahead of that. I didn't take a red-eye cross-country for one date. Or even for some between-the-sheets action, although I'm sure as fuck not going to object if we wind up naked and sweaty. I'm already up to the damn hearts and flowers he dismissed so casually.

Baby steps, Casanova. Baby steps.

His fingers thread through mine, and he turns his head to catch me staring at him. I should be embarrassed but I'm not because the hunger in his eyes matches what I'm sure is reflected in my own. It's real. Raw. Almost a living, breathing thing, pulsing between us.

"Shouldn't you be watching the ballet?" he whispers, his eyes not leaving mine.

"Shouldn't you?" I hold his gaze. The pulsing is so strong it physically hurts a little. But at the same time, it feels so good. Good to know the attraction isn't one-sided. That the zing we had in college is still there, at least on some level.

"This is your party," he says, his tongue stealing out to moisten his lips. "You're the dancer."

Cheeks scorching, I fight the urge to throw my high-minded notion to wait for David to make the first move out the window. It's the lip licking. It's like an open invitation to plant my mouth on his. But I've been there, done that last night, and I want tonight to end differently. So I tear my eyes off those infuriatingly tempting, way-too-kissable lips and stick to my game plan.

"I've seen *Giselle*. I'd rather watch you."

"Creeper."

The word would hurt if it wasn't for the smile that accompanies it, reaching out and enveloping me through the darkness. I'm strangely content, cocooned in a haze of sweet sexual tension—until he slips his fingers from mine.

My body screams in protest at the loss of contact, but it's not screaming for long. His hand moves to my thigh, slowly inching toward the growing bulge between my legs until it's only centimeters from my dick. It twitches in anticipation, and I silently will him to wrap those long, nimble pianist's fingers around it and stroke. Pump. Squeeze. Something, anything to relieve this pressure, this ache that only he can satisfy.

It's decadent. Dangerous. I know some people get off on public sex. The risk of getting caught gives them a thrill. It's never been my thing, but I'm starting to see the appeal.

"Please," I hiss just as the lights come up and he jerks his hand back.

Fuck. Intermission.

"Intermission," he says, echoing my thoughts. He stands abruptly, almost falling over himself in his rush to escape the box. "Bathroom break. Be right back."

He disappears through the curtains and I'm left stewing in uncertainty, my cock at half-mast and still throbbing. Did he mean it when he said he'd be right back? Or did he cut and run? I don't know whether to follow him and make sure he's okay or give him some space to figure things out on his own.

I'm not a fucking mind reader, unfortunately, so there are no easy answers. I'm just going to have to trust my gut. And my gut's telling me to go after him—as soon as my damn dick calms down and I'm not sporting a woody.

I adjust my fly and try some surefire erection killers. Like counting to one hundred by threes. Reciting the preamble to the Constitution. Picturing my third-grade teacher, Mrs. Bindus, naked. But I'm still hard as a steel pipe when the curtains part and David waltzes through.

"Here." He tosses me a pack of candy. "I saw these at the concession stand and thought of you."

I flip it over in my hand and smile. "Gummy worms?"

He shrugs and sits. "They're your favorite, right?"

"Yeah." I clear my throat. I'm getting choked up. Over a bag of fruit-flavored gelatin shaped like invertebrates. Could I be any more pathetic? "I can't believe you remembered."

"How could I forget? You practically lived on them. Your mom used to send them to you in bulk." He glances down at my lap, where my cock is still straining against my zipper, and swallows hard. Damn, even his Adam's apple is sexy. "Did I do that?"

My first instinct is to try to hide my obvious erection, but I stop myself. No use denying his effect on me when the evidence is staring him in the face. I rip open the bag of gummies, pop a green one in my mouth, and hold the bag out to David. "I guess some things haven't changed since college."

"Since college?" he echoes, waving off the candy.

I hunt through the bag for an orange one—they're the best, no matter what anyone else says—and slurp it down. "Yeah. I might not have wanted to admit it back then, but I had a huge-ass crush on you. I used to stalk the practice rooms, hoping to run into you."

"No way."

"Way."

"All this time I thought it was my music you liked." He gives me a shy smile that fades as quickly as it appears. "I mean, that one time we kissed, you couldn't get away fast enough. And the next week at graduation, Sonja had a ring on her finger."

Yeah. Not my finest hour. I force myself to look right at him, so he can see the sincerity in my eyes when I apologize. Again.

Not that I mind. I'll apologize a hundred times over if that's what it takes for him to trust me. "That was a dick move. I was afraid of what I was feeling. So I took the easy way out. Or what seemed like the easy way at the time."

But denying my sexual orientation had been anything but easy. Eventually it became impossible, and denying changed to hiding. Lying. Sneaking around. Jerking off to gay porn when Sonja was out with her girlfriends. Surfing Grindr on my cell phone, half wishing I could work up the nerve to do more than just scroll through the profiles of guys looking to hook up. It was like living two separate lives—one public, the other private, neither satisfying.

"I get it." David shrugs and steals a gummy. "You weren't ready to come out. Maybe you're still not ready. It's a personal decision. One only you can make."

I reach across the armrest and grab his hand. Even though I'm pretty sure no one can see it, there's something about the gesture that seems important. Emotionally charged. A sign of wanting to be close, and not just in a sexual way. "If I wasn't ready, I wouldn't be here."

The lights flicker, signaling that intermission is almost over and the second act is about to begin. Dammit. Just as our conversation is getting good. Talk about shitty timing.

I suck down one last worm and fold the bag over. I'm sticking it into my inside jacket pocket when David leans closer and whispers in my ear, his hot breath caressing my skin.

"Do you want to get out of here?"

Cue the goose bumps.

A muscle tics in my jaw. "Don't you want to know what

happens to Albrecht and Giselle?"

"You can fill me in on the cab ride." He stands, holding out a hand to me. I take it almost reflexively, and he yanks me to my feet. His grip is sure and strong and warm, steadying my shaky nerves.

"What cab ride?" I ask, my voice thick.

He weaves his fingers between mine, making it impossible for me to pull away. If I wanted to. Which I don't.

"To my place."

-Chapter Three-

David

This is either the best move I've ever made or the stupidest. It's sure as fuck the boldest. *No risk, no reward,* I remind myself as Chris hails a cab, which pulls to a stop at the curb in front of us.

"514 East 5th Street, please," I instruct the cabbie as I slide into the back seat.

"The Village?" Chris slides in next to me and pulls the door shut. "Sweet."

It is. My tiny, third-floor walk-up is nothing fancy, but it's mine. No roommate. No hour-long commute from Brooklyn. It's taken me almost five years and more auditions, self-tapes, and resume drop-offs than I can count to get to this point. I may not have hit the big time yet, but I'm busting my ass to get there, and I'm working steadily enough to afford the exorbitant Manhattan rent for the first time since moving to the Big Apple.

I wonder if that's why I suggested we go to my place and not Chris's hotel room. To show Chris what a good catch I am. That I may not be a world-traveled *danseur noble,* but I've done okay for myself. That I'm worthy of him, as worthy as any of the handsome, hard-bodied dancers he works with on a daily basis.

If only I believed that myself.

"You got awfully quiet," he says, biting his lip. Fuck, that's sexy. My dick feels heavy and full. "Having second thoughts?"

"No." I put a palm on his forearm and squeeze. Touching him, even somewhere as innocuous as his arm, feels good. Feels right. I want this—us—so bad, I literally ache for it. "Far from it."

"Thank fuck. You scared me for a minute there."

My hand glides up to his shoulder. His muscles are tight, hard knots under my fingers. "Damn, you're tense. Sure you're not the one with second thoughts?"

"Hell, no." He does that sexy lip biting thing again. Now my cock's like a goddamn lead weight in my pants. "Just nervous."

"Well, you can't smoke to calm yourself down this time," I say, half teasing. "It's against the law in New York City cabs. But maybe I can do something to help you relax."

"Oh, yeah?" His shy smile turns seductive and his eyes get heavy-lidded and dark with desire. "Like what?"

I know where his dirty mind is going, but I'm not quite there yet. Okay, that's a lie. I'm there, but I don't want to rush things. It's his first time. With a guy, that is. It should be special. Something he'll never forget. Whatever happens after tonight, at least I can give him that. And me, if I'm honest. I like knowing that even if I'm not his last, I'll always be his first.

"Turn around."

He blinks, confused. "Huh?"

"You heard me. Turn around."

He does, and I put both my hands on his shoulders, grip them hard, and dig in with my thumbs, working out the stiffness in his neck and upper back.

He groans and lets his head fall onto his chest. "Not exactly where I thought this was going, but . . ."

His voice tails off into another groan as my thumbs work on a particularly tough knot.

"We'll get to that." I massage my way toward the center of his back, between his shoulder blades. "Eventually."

Just not in the cramped, cracked-vinyl back seat of an aging yellow cab with the equally aging driver checking us out in his rearview mirror every chance he gets.

"Holy shit that feels fantastic," Chris mumbles into his chest.

I can't help myself. I lean down and kiss the back of his neck, not caring if the cabbie's sneaking a peak at us. Let him look. A little kiss never hurt anyone. "Magic piano fingers, remember?"

He lifts his head and shoots me a hungry look over his shoulder. "You realize all this is doing is making me even more horny."

"All? What about my skills as a masseuse? This is professional-level attention you're getting here. You can't tell me it's not loosening you up."

My fingers inch down his spine to his lower back, just above his waistband. I'm dying to rip off his suit jacket and pull his dress shirt from his fancy pants, to work my hands underneath and feel bare skin under my fingertips. But I'm not willing to give the cab driver that much of a show, so skin-on-skin will have to take a back seat. Pun intended.

"You know what I mean," he says on a moan. "I fucking need you. Now. I'm not going to be able to wait until we get to your place."

The cab jerks to stop, and I drop my hands to whip out my

wallet. But it's okay because I know in a few minutes I'll have him exactly where I want him. Where I've always wanted him. All to myself. At my mercy. "You don't have to. We're here."

I pay the cab driver, and we make it up the three floors in half my usual time. The second we're inside, he's on me, panting like he's run a marathon as he shoves me back against the door and presses his body against mine.

Fuck, he feels fantastic. I want to let him have his way with me. Let him strip my clothes off and kiss me senseless. But not yet. Me first. And by that, I mean I'm going to make him come first, not vice versa.

"Whoa there, ballet boy." He's strong from years of dancing, and it takes all my reserve to push him away. "I appreciate your enthusiasm. But that's not how this is gonna go."

"How is it gonna go, then?"

"Like a rhumba," I say, speaking his language. The language of dance. "Slow and smooth and sensuous. Not some herky-jerky, quick-and-dirty hip-hop routine."

"What's wrong with quick and dirty?" he grumbles.

"Not a damn thing, in the right circumstances."

"And this isn't the right circumstances?"

"Hell, no," I growl, looking up at him to meet his heated gaze. He's got a couple of inches on me with that long, lean body. "Your intro to gay sex is not going to be a fast and furious fuck against my front door."

"Even if that's what I want?"

"It might be what you want. But it's not what you need."

He lets out a frustrated howl that goes straight to my cock. "I so want to hate you right now."

"You won't in a few minutes."

I take his hand and lead him into the living room. I'm hoping we'll get to the bedroom eventually, but it's too soon for that. Too presumptuous. My second-hand leather couch will do for now. It's a decent compromise between my bed and the damn door.

"Sit," I instruct him, my voice coming out sharper than I expect. Damn. You learn something new every day. Who knew I could do bossy gay? I guess Chris brings out the dom in me.

He lowers himself to the sofa, and I follow him down, sitting next to him and taking his head in my hands. For a long second we just sit there silently, staring at each other, our warm breath mingling in the small space between our lips.

"What the fuck are you waiting for?" Chris rasps. "Kiss me already."

I move in, and he tenses a little, like he's bracing himself for another taste of my lips. But I fake him out, going for his neck instead of his mouth. His skin is a delicious combination of salty and sweet, like a chocolate-covered pretzel, and I wonder if his dick tastes as good. Or better.

"Tease," he murmurs as I drop hungry, open-mouthed kisses from his jaw to his collarbone.

I peel off his jacket, unbutton his shirt and spread it open so my lips can continue their journey south, giving me a first look at his naked chest. Damn, those pecs. And his abs. Holy hell. Is that an eight-pack? I thought they only existed in Marvel movies. And porno films.

I pull back, more than a little self-conscious of my own less-than-perfect body. Don't get me wrong. I'm not a total couch potato. I work out a few times a week. Try to eat right. But Chris is on another level. The guy doesn't have an ounce of fat on him. Anywhere. There's no way I can live up to that.

"Hey," he says, his voice low and husky. "Where do you think you're going? You're not backing out on me, are you?"

"No. Not really. It's just—" I break off, my face flushed with embarrassment.

"Just what?" A frown mars his movie-star good looks. "Was it something I said? Or did? I admit, I'm a little out of practice. Plus, I've never actually done this before. You know, with a guy."

"No," I insist too loudly. The idea that he thinks my hang-ups are his problem—that I've done something to make him feel that way—tears at my gut like a knife. A serrated knife with a rusty blade. I'm supposed to be the experienced one, the one putting him at ease, not the other way around.

I take a deep, steadying breath and make a conscious effort to soften my tone. "It's not you. It's me. I know that sounds trite, but it's true. You're so goddamn beautiful. I can't compete with all that."

"All what?"

"That." I wave a hand at his naked torso. "The sculpted pecs. The washboard abs. You're a professional ballet dancer. I'm a piano player who spends his days—and nights—sitting on his ass at the keyboard. I'm afraid you're going to be disappointed when my clothes hit the floor."

"The only way you could disappoint me is if your clothes stayed on." He tilts his head to one side, eyeing me with the piercing gaze of a master painter studying his favorite muse. "Remember the night we met?"

"Huh?" The abrupt change of subject jars me. Now it's my

turn to be confused. I'm not sure where he's going with this.

"The night we met," he repeats, removing his shirt and leaning back, strong, sinewy arms crossed behind his head. He probably figures the less clothes he's wearing, the less likely I'll be able to resist jumping his bones. Smart man. "Freshman year. At that epic musical theater club keg party."

"I'm pretty sure I noticed you before that," I say, finding it hard to tear my gaze from his bare chest. His evil plan is clearly working. "At mass on Sundays."

I went every week. Not out of some great religious devotion, despite what my parents wanted to think. I went to ogle the cute seminarians. And Chris. Sinful, I know. Guaranteed it's earned me a special place in hell.

He shakes his head, and his lips curve into a youthful, mischievous grin that's reminiscent of the boy I lusted after from my favorite pew in the back of St. Cecilia's. "That doesn't count. I'm talking about when we actually met. As in exchanged words. Had a conversation."

"The keg party." It's all coming back to me now. Truth is, it never left. If I close my eyes, I can almost see him back then, a little younger, a little lankier, a little more awkward in the way of an adolescent male just getting used to his developing body, skinny jeans and tight T-shirt practically painted onto his slender frame and a red Solo cup filled with whatever cheap beer was on tap clutched in one hand.

But I don't close my eyes for more than a few seconds because that means depriving myself of the sight of him now. Half naked. "Right. That crazy violinist wouldn't leave you alone."

"Renee." He rolls his eyes and grimaces. "With the grabby

hands.”

“She was all over you,” I say on a laugh. “And a terrible violinist. To this day, I don’t understand how she ever got past the audition.”

He sits up and puts both hands flat on my chest, his eyes laser beams, boring into mine. “I didn’t bring up that night so we could reminisce about Crazy Renee.”

My breath hitches and I’m pretty sure he can feel my heart jumping around in my rib cage like it’s trying to escape. “Then why did you bring it up?”

“Because I wanted you to kiss me,” he says, nervously toying with the top button of my shirt. “After you rescued me from Renee and we brought that bottle of Boone’s Farm we found in the fridge up to the roof of the dancers’ dorm. I was too scared to make the first move. But that didn’t stop me from hoping you would.”

“I almost did,” I admit, a little stunned by his revelation. And by the way he’s slipping my button out of its hole. “But I didn’t want to take advantage of you when you were drunk. Then when I did finally kiss you—”

“Years later,” he interrupts, his trembling fingers moving down to the next button.

“You freaked out and ran back to your girlfriend.”

Button number two pops free. “A lot had changed by then.”

“Yeah.” His fingers graze the trail of hair that bisects my chest as they move lower, and my breath catches again. “You were dating Sonja.”

“And you’d stuck me permanently in the friend zone. Or so I thought.”

I let my head fall back against the couch. "We wasted so much time."

"Let's not waste any more." The last button gives way and he drops his hands. "Take off your shirt. I promise I won't run away this time."

"Very funny."

"There's nothing funny about this." He palms the noticeable bulge in his pants.

Holy mandingo. That's got to be at least eight inches he's packing. My body hums with anticipation as I whip off my shirt and toss it behind me, not even caring where it lands.

Chris reaches for me, tentatively at first then a bit more forcefully, pulling me in. Then he's kissing me and oh my God he's good at this. I kiss him back, making soft, encouraging noises as I open up to him. His tongue darts inside and I suck on it greedily, loving the taste, the feel of him.

Unlike both our prior encounters, we're in this kiss together from the start. That alone makes it ten thousand times better than anything in my admittedly limited sexual experience.

"Fuck." The word comes out on a gasp as his hands explore my shoulders, my spine, the small of my back. I wrap my arms around him and yank him closer to me, bringing us bare chest to bare chest.

The contact makes my dick do a little happy dance. Chris must feel it because he grinds against me like a stripper, rubbing his throbbing cock against mine. The friction has me seconds away from coming in my goddamn pants.

"Someone's impatient tonight," I rasp. "Pretty bold for a first-timer."

His hands freeze on my ass. "Is that a problem?"

A randy shiver races through me and another rush of blood floods my already engorged cock. "No. No problem. Be as bold as you like."

But don't be surprised if I last all of two minutes—and that's being generous—before I shoot my load.

He stands suddenly, awkwardly, one hand hesitating then going to his fly. He's trying so hard to be daring. Confident. I want to tell him he doesn't have to. That I don't want him to be or do anything that's out of his comfort zone. But I get the feeling he's got something he has to prove—to himself, not to me—so I sit back and wait it out as he adorably fumbles with his fly.

After a few tries, he pops the button with shaky fingers and slowly slides the zipper down. Then he works a hand inside his pants and runs it over the navy blue cotton of his boxers, stroking his monster dick through the fabric.

I lick my lips, almost involuntarily. "If you're trying to kill me before we get started, you're doing a great job."

"I don't want to kill you." He hooks his thumbs into his waistband and shoves his pants over his hips and down his legs. When they reach his ankles, he kicks them off, leaving him in only his formfitting boxer briefs.

Damn. My mouth goes dry and my brain cells short circuit. He really is going to kill me. But at least I'll die happy.

"Then what do you want?" I ask. I need to know. And I need him to be specific. And certain. Once we do this, there's no going back.

"I—I want you naked." He jerks himself through his boxers. Whether he's aware of it or not, he's putting on a show for me. My living room is his stage, and I'm his audience of one. "And I want to suck you off."

"Yes and no," I answer, and his face falls, his disappointment almost palpable. But that's okay. I know it won't last for long.

"What's that mean?" he asks.

"Yes, I'll get naked. But no, you can't suck me off. Not yet." I stand, strip, and cross to him, sinking to my knees. My eyes are level with his cock, and I reach up to cup it, pushing his hand out of the way. "This is my apartment. You're my guest tonight. And company comes first."

-Chapter Four-

Chris

Company comes first.

Hands down the three hottest words I've ever heard. Even hotter because they're from the mouth of the guy who's fueled my gay sex fantasies since I allowed myself to have gay sex fantasies. And who's kneeling in front of me, gloriously naked, freeing my swollen cock from my boxer briefs.

Holy shit. He wasn't kidding when he said he had magic fingers. They sure know their way around a guy's dick. The way he strokes me is faster, firmer, rougher than a woman's touch.

I like it. No, that's a lie. I fucking love it.

His free hand travels up my thigh and over my hip, coming to rest against the eight-pack I work hard in the gym to maintain. "Man. You have zero body hair."

"Occupational hazard," I grunt. "Minimalist costumes and muscle bears don't mix well."

"You're ripped, but you're not jacked enough to be a muscle bear. You're more of an otter. Or a jock." Okay. Guess I still have a lot to learn about LGBTQ slang. But that will have to wait. Right now I'm having a hard time focusing on anything except his wandering fingers, teasing the area where my happy trail would be if I didn't wax regularly.

He moves in closer as he continues to jerk me off, and his soft, shallow breaths tickle my dick. "But it's totally hot. All that smooth, shiny skin waiting to be explored."

His tongue comes out to lap up a bead of precum at the tip of my aching cock, and damn if that slippery little sucker isn't as magic as his fingers. I inhale sharply, every fiber of my being vibrating with sexual energy and raw need.

"Fuck. Do that again."

"You want my mouth?" he asks, sitting back on his haunches, which increases the distance between his lips and my dick.

Bastard.

"Fuck, yes," I moan, not too proud to beg. "Please."

"I can't resist when you ask nicely."

He wraps his hand around the base of my cock, his grip firm and sure, and those sinful lips part as he brings his mouth nearer, nearer, until it's around my head, warm and wet. He licks one, two, three slow circles around the tip then sucks me in deeper, his tongue teasing the underside of my shaft.

Fuckity fuck fuck fuck. I grit my teeth and concentrate on not shooting off like a goddamn cruise missile. I will not embarrass myself. I've waited too long for this for it to end in a matter of minutes.

But David seems determined to prove me wrong. He swallows me whole, and I feel my cock hit the back of his throat. My knees buckle, and I groan in protest when he pulls off me.

"Couch." He points behind me. "Sit."

It's a good thing it's only a few steps away because I'm not sure my shaky legs will carry me much farther. I sink down onto one of the leather cushions, and within seconds David's between my thighs, pushing them apart so he can dive back in and devour me some more.

I watch him through half-closed eyes and my hands drift downward to cup his head, his thick, silky hair sliding through my fingers. "Holy hell, dude. I think you're the one who's trying to kill me."

He raises his head and releases me with a loud pop. "Enjoying your inaugural blow job from a guy?"

"I'm not sure enjoying is the right word." My hips buck, telling him without words that I need his mouth on me again. I've never felt so out of control. And it's fucking awesome. Control is overrated. A little submission every once in a while doesn't make a man any less of a man, no matter if he's gay, straight, or anything in between. "I might pass out if I don't come soon."

He doesn't answer, just ducks his head and takes me in again. My toes curl and my fingers grasp at his hair like it's a lifeline as he wrecks me with his lips, teeth, and tongue. I don't have another guy to compare him to, but I don't need one to know that he is seriously, seriously good at this.

I want like hell to make it last, but that's so not gonna happen. Not with the way my cock is pulsing and my heart is pounding. Then there are the sounds David is making. Muffled groans, wet slurps, and rhythmic grunts that take me to the edge of the cliff, mere millimeters from tumbling into oblivion.

"Gotta come," I warn him. "Watch out."

But instead of pulling back so I can blow my load in his hand or on his chest, he doubles down, groaning louder and sucking me all the way down to the root, his chin bumping my balls. My hips twitch and my back arches and I pour myself into him.

He takes every last drop, and when I'm done my whole body goes slack and my head flops back against the couch, eyes closed. I'm shaking and spent and thoroughly satisfied, unable to do anything but sit there like a limp noodle and marinate in the memory of how my college crush just gave me the best blow job of my life.

But David's still ready and raring to go. I hear him get up from the floor and feel the couch cushion next to me sink with his weight. Then he's taking my hand, putting it on what feels like—holy crap, is that his dick?

My head snaps up and my eyes fly open. Yep. It's his dick all right. In my hand. I've never held a guy's dick before, obviously. It's thick and heavy and pointing straight up, pressed against his belly and leaking precum on his rippled abs.

I don't know what the hell he was worried about. He's got absolutely no reason to be self-conscious. He may not have the insane definition of a dancer's body—hell, few people do, and it's nearly impossible to maintain—but it's obvious he works out. His stomach is flat, his biceps are firm, and his thighs and calves are toned and taut.

And his goddamn cock is a thing of beauty. Long and pink and smooth, capped with a mushroom head that I'm dying to put my lips around. Without really thinking about it, my fingers form a tight circle and I give it a long, slow stroke.

"That's it." He thrusts up into my hand. "Harder. Don't be afraid to be a little rough."

I hesitate, my grip on him loosening. The polar opposite of

what he asked for. But never having done this before, I'm overly cautious. I know how I like to be touched, but I'm not sure how that translates into me touching another dude's dick. "I don't want to hurt you."

He reaches down and closes his hand around mine. His cock throbs, hot and hard in my fingers. "Don't worry. I'll tell you if it's too much. I want to watch you jack me off."

Who am I to deny the man what he wants? I slide my hand down his shaft, over the head and back to the base. And because I like having my balls played with, I decide to go lower, cupping his in my palm and squeezing.

His already dark eyes grow even darker as he lifts his hips to make it easier for me to fondle him. "Keep that up and I won't last long."

"No fair. You're not allowed to come. Not before I taste you."

I lean over and touch my lips to the tip of his dick. My tongue flicks the slit that runs down the middle, and I get my first taste of guy goo. It's warm and slightly salty, like saltwater taffy.

My first thought is how easily I could become addicted to it, a prospect that's equal parts thrilling and terrifying. My second is that I don't care how fucking frightening it is, there's no way I'm leaving this apartment without returning the favor and swallowing everything he has to give me.

"Cocktease." David nudges his hips upward again, lifting his fine ass off the couch. "Stop torturing me and suck it already."

He doesn't have to ask me twice. "Your command is my wish."

His cock is stiff and dripping. For me. I brush my lips across the head and rub the shaft against my cheek, teasing him one last time with my five o'clock shadow before I open wide and put him out of his misery.

"Fuck," he moans. "Need this. Need you."

His words make my heart happy, and my lips curve into a smile around his dick. I suck him in deeper and deeper, trying to fit his entire length into my mouth. I can't quite get there. Yet.

But he doesn't seem to mind my lack of experience. I must be doing something right because he comes in mere minutes, bucking and writhing and muttering incoherently as he floods my mouth with the saltwater taffy taste of his orgasm.

When he's done, I raise my head and plant a kiss in the middle of his sweat-dampened chest, where a fine trail of dark hair bisects his abs. David reciprocates, kissing my collarbone, then gathers me to him and stretches out on the couch, taking me down with him. His arms band around me and he buries his face in my neck.

Wow. David's a snuggler. Who knew?

Fortunately, so am I. We lie there, legs tangled, holding each other as our panting subsides and our heart rates return to normal, and it's fucking heaven. I'm so blissed out I don't even care that his couch really isn't big enough for the two of us and I'll probably wind up with a stiff neck and sore back.

"Sorry," he murmurs against my throat. "I should have warned you I was about to blow."

Apology totally unnecessary. He's crazy if he thinks he's getting any complaints from me. It wasn't like a warning was going to change anything. He blew exactly where I wanted him to blow.

"It's okay." My words are slow and slurred. Now that we've

both gotten off, exhaustion is starting to creep in. "I didn't mind."

He nuzzles the spot behind my ear and inhales. Did he just sniff me? I hope I smell like Nautica Voyage and not postcoital funk.

"Are you sure you've never done this before?" he asks. "You're awfully good for a novice."

"I'm pretty sure I'd remember if I had."

"I'm pretty sure you would, too."

He chuckles, and the sound reverberates through me, making my heart swell like the Grinch's when he finally figures out the true meaning of Christmas. If the sex was mind-blowing—and it was—this—the after-sex cuddling and pillow talk —is something even bigger. It's soul-shaking.

My eyelids droop as I relax into him, fighting to suppress a yawn. But it's a losing battle. As much as I want to stay awake and savor every second tangled up with David, exhaustion is winning this one, hands down.

I feel his fingertips skate over my jawline, through the long-past-five-o'clock stubble that dots my face. "You know, my bed is way bigger. And way more comfortable."

"I'll bet," I murmur, not opening my now fully closed eyes.

"Wanna move this party to the bedroom?"

"Okay."

But that doesn't happen. We fall asleep on the couch, wrapped up in each other.

Eventually, we make it to the bed. There are more blow jobs, and at one point David gets bold enough to slip a finger between my ass cheeks, penetrating me with the tip. The sensation is unfamiliar but not unpleasant. A slight burn that gradually morphs into a kind of pleasure I've never felt before.

After a few minutes, he starts to slowly work it in further, even adding another finger to the mix. My thigh muscles tremble and I push against him, wanting more. But no matter how much I beg him, he won't fuck me.

"Not yet," he says. Again. "You're not ready to bottom. I don't want to hurt you."

"Then let me fuck you," I demand.

He flips over on his stomach so fast I burst out laughing. That's another thing I didn't expect. Sex with David isn't just hot. It's hysterical. We laugh as much as we moan. There's a comfort level between us that five years apart hasn't tempered. It makes the sex easy. Fun. Like riding a bike, but with orgasms.

I mimic how he touched me, sliding a finger down his crease, then stop. I have no fucking clue what I'm doing. And just like he doesn't want to hurt me, I don't want to hurt him. "You're going to have to talk me through this."

"There's lube in the top drawer of the nightstand." He sticks his ass up in the air and wiggles it temptingly. As if I need any additional enticement to tap that. "And condoms."

I spend the next half hour learning how David likes to be fucked. First with one finger, then two. Finding his prostate, watching his face contort and hearing his sexy whimpers and moans. He grinds his ass against my probing finger, trying to fuck it, and pride swells my chest. Whatever I'm doing, I must be doing it right.

Then, finally, it's my dick inside him, pushing past the tight ring of muscle and burying myself in that fine ass of his. Fuck, it's tight. The pressure is beyond anything I've ever felt before. He's like a hot, wet vise, squeezing me into next week.

It'll be a miracle if I last more than a few strokes. But I'm going to give it the old college try.

I bend down, covering his body with mine, and start to move.

"Wait." The word is like a pinprick to my stupid pride. Maybe I'm not so great at this after all. "Flip me over. I wanna look at you when you're fucking me."

Just like that, my pride is restored. He wants to watch me. Gaze into my eyes while I make love to him. Because that's what I'll be doing. Making love. This is no fast, forgettable fuck for me. And I'm starting to think maybe it's not for him, either. "Uh, yeah. I'd like that, too."

We switch positions so he's on his back with me looming above him, braced on my palms, one on either side of his head. "You ready?"

He nods, his sex-mussed hair drooping into his eyes. He's so goddamn beautiful, helpless underneath me, his cheeks flushed and his eyes glassy with undisguised lust. "I've been ready since the first time I saw you."

Holy hell. He talks as pretty as he looks. If I'm not back inside him in the next thirty seconds, I might die. I grab my iron-hard cock and position myself at his entrance. "Sorry it took me so long to catch up."

"Better late than never," he says, a bemused smile curving the corners of his full, kissable lips. It takes me a second to get the joke. Then I remember. It's the same thing I said to him when I asked him out.

"Told you so." The tip of my dick nudges his hole.

"Come on, ballet boy. Do it."

I ease in. Just the head at first, then I'm all the way in, teasing him with slow, easy strokes.

"Faster," he pleads, wrapping his legs around my back and sneaking a hand between us to search for his cock.

I slap his hand away. "Nice try, but I don't need any help. I'm making you come."

"Then do it already."

I curl my fingers around his shaft and give it a quick, hard pump just as I thrust back into him. He's right. It's better this way. Face to face, I get the full force of his expressions. The way he bites his lip to keep from crying out. The strain on his handsome features. The sweat dampening his brow.

He's close, and so am I. Just like when he blew me on the couch, I want to hold off my release, but that would be like asking the Patriots not to win the Super Bowl.

My orgasm is relentless. It rips through me, red-hot and pulsing, like a series of power surges, and I empty myself inside him, still jerking him off.

David follows right after me, drenching my fingers with his sticky seed. He comes for what seems like forever. When he's finally still, I collapse next to him with a low, drawn-out groan.

He throws one leg over my hip, pinning our sweaty bodies together. We lay like that for a while, not speaking, just clinging to each other, until David finally breaks the silence. "So what's the verdict?"

"What verdict?"

"Doing a dude. Was it all you'd hoped it would be?"

It was. That and more. But I'm not sure he's ready for me to confess my undying love for him after one roll in the hay, so I just kiss his damp neck. Fuck, I love the taste of him. I was right about him being addictive.

Hi, my name is Chris, and I'm a David-aholic.

"Ten out of ten stars," I say, kissing him again.

We return to our companionable postorgasm silence. After a few minutes, David rolls away from me and heads for the adjoining bathroom, and my mind immediately jumps to the worst possible conclusion.

"Do you want me to go?" I call after him, propping myself up on one elbow.

"Only if you want to," he says, coming back into the room with two towels. He tosses one to me and wipes his abs with the other. "Thought you might like to clean up."

"Oh." I sit up and run the towel over my stomach and groin. "Thanks."

He drops his towel and climbs back into bed. "It's still early. We could catch a few more hours of sleep. Maybe grab some breakfast when we wake up. If that works for you."

"Yeah, that works." As much as I'd like to stay like this for the next ten or twenty years or so, I have to go back to San Fran tomorrow. But my flight's not until late afternoon, so I'll settle for breakfast. For now.

I toss my towel onto the floor and lie down next to him. He nudges me onto my side so my back is to his chest. Then he wraps an arm around my waist and strokes lazy circles on my stomach with his hand. And we're still that way when we drift off to sleep.

-Chapter Five-

David

"All right, that's it. I can't keep my mouth shut any longer."

Denice, my favorite waitress, sits her ass down on the piano bench next to me. The boss glares at her from behind the bar, but she waves him off. It's a slow night. The handful of current patrons are contentedly sipping their cocktails. And if anyone else comes in, she'll see them from here.

"Since when have you ever kept your mouth shut?" I mutter.

"I heard that." She sticks her tongue out at me. Very ladylike. Very mature. Totally Denice. "And you'll pay for it later. But right now, I want to know what's going on with you. Spill."

"Spill what?" I ask as I launch into a new song. Carole King. Not my usual jam, but I'm feeling a little maudlin.

"The reason you're depressed."

What the actual fuck? Is Denice a mind reader? Or have I been that obvious? "Who says I'm depressed?"

"You do, that's who." She elbows me in the ribs. Hard. That's the kind of relationship we've got. She's like the annoying but lovable little sister I never had.

Me being the professional I am, I don't miss a beat, my hands continuing to fly across the keys, a blur of black and white under my fingers. "I don't know what you're talking about."

She gives me a sympathetic side-eyed look. "'Ain't No Sunshine.' 'Home.' 'You're So Far Away.' It's obvious from your song selection that you're missing someone."

That's the understatement of the year. Maybe even the decade. It's been two weeks since Chris blew back into my life like a Category 5 hurricane. Two of the longest weeks of my young life.

True, it's not like he blew in and then blew back out again without a trace. It doesn't look like he's planning on ghosting me this time around. We've kept in touch, even after he jetted back to the Left Coast the day after we hooked up. There have been hundreds of texts, almost daily phone calls, even a couple of very memorable—and very dirty—Skype chats. And we've talked about getting together again soon, either on his side of the continent or mine.

But none of that is enough when you've finally found—or refound, I guess would be more accurate—the right guy. The one you've known you wanted to spend the rest of your life with pretty much since the day you laid eyes on him. I defy anyone who doesn't believe in love at first sight to convince me otherwise.

"Hello." Denice raps on my head with her fist. "Earth to David."

"Don't you have customers to take care of?" I ask, knowing full well she's got everything under control.

"Not at the moment." She flips her hair over her shoulder and scoots closer to me, practically forcing me off the bench. "Is this about that hottie who came to hear you play? You've been brooding ever since you disappeared into the alley with him."

She noticed? I should have counted on that. I thought we were pretty discreet, but sometimes Denice is way too observant for her own good. It's a great quality for a waitress. Not so great when you're trying to fly under her radar.

"Of course I noticed," she says with another hair flip. *Damn.* I didn't realize I said that aloud. So much for keeping my inner monologue on the inside. "You hate having visitors while you're working. But you made an exception for him. I figured he must be someone special."

I can't stop my fingers from slipping on the keyboard this time, producing a discordant mess for a hot second. I hate keeping secrets from my friends. But how am I supposed to tell Denice about Chris when I'm not even sure where I stand with him? And how are he and I supposed to maintain a relationship—if that's even what this is—when we're 3,000 miles apart?

I've got lots of questions, but no answers. So I say nothing, regain my composure, and muddle my way through the last bars of Carole's haunting melody. I'm not singing, but that doesn't stop the lyrics from echoing in my head.

And it doesn't help to know you're so far away.

Yeah, you're so far away.

Denice is right. It's damn depressing. The end of the song is greeted with scattered applause from the sparse crowd, and I purposely choose a more upbeat song—"Copacabana"—for my next number. That ought to throw her off track. Plus, I need the practice. Rumor has it the Barry Manilow jukebox musical's looking for a new pianist. I'm going to drop off my resume at the stage door in the morning.

"Nice try," she says, not falling for my diversionary tactic for one second. "But you're not getting out of this that easily. It's going to take more than a change of tempo to distract me."

But thankfully that's all she gets the chance to say because a group of six walks in and sits down at a table in the corner. Probably the start of the after-theater crowd if their cocktail dresses and sports coats—and the Playbills in their hands—are anything to go by.

Denice stands with a resigned sigh. "I mean it. My shift will be over when your last set's done. We can grab a few drinks and an order of nachos supreme at Macho Taco. And you can tell me all about your mystery man."

"We'll see," I hedge, focusing on my playing to avoid meeting her eyes. Otherwise, she'll know the excuses I'm about to hand her are complete bullshit And she's already seen through me enough for one night. "I'm kind of tired. And I've got a lot of stuff to catch up on at home."

"Like what?" she calls over her shoulder as she heads off to wait on the new arrivals. "Organize your sock drawer?"

"My sock drawer is a work of art."

"I'll bet it is."

The familiar, very masculine voice doesn't belong to Denice. Now my fingers don't just slip. They stall, and the music stalls with them. I look up from the keyboard to see Chris, lounging against the piano like he's about to belt out a torch song.

"Chris. You're . . . here."

Real smooth, ex-lax. But it's the best my mouth can manage. Hell, I'm shocked it managed that. Chris is back. Looking motherfucking mouthwatering in slim-fit jeans and a lavender polo shirt that brings out the green in his hazel eyes. It's enough to render a man speechless.

He flashes me a thousand-watt smile, making my already dry mouth feel like the Sahara. "Surprise."

"You can say that again."

His gaze darts down to my hands, still motionless on the keyboard, then back up to my face. "Shouldn't you be playing something? I don't want to get you in trouble."

"Right." And now that the shock of seeing him is wearing off and my brain is starting to function again, I know just the song.

"'As Time Goes By.'" He nods, somehow fitting his hands inside the pockets of his tight jeans. "Excellent choice."

Score one for the piano man. My mouth may have dropped the ball, but I can always count on my fingers to do the talking. "Of all the gin joints, in all the towns, in all the world. . ."

"I walk into yours." His eyes flick to the other side of the room, where my boss is glaring at us from across the massive mahogany bar. "Can we talk?"

The three most ominous words in the English language. Does anything good ever come after them? I'm hoping whatever Chris wants to say is the exception and not the rule.

Either way, I need to know. But now's not the time. I need this job. My rent won't pay itself.

I shake my head. "I've got to finish this set."

"Consider it finished." This comes from Denice, who's materialized from who knows where at Chris's elbow. She gives him a quick once-over and shoots me a not-so-subtle thumbs-up from behind his back. "Take a break. I'll run interference for you with the evil overlord."

"Are you sure?"

"Sure, I'm sure. I'll tell him hottie here"—she pats Chris on the arm, and I swear her hand lingers a little too long so she can cop a feel of his beefy biceps—"is your long-lost cousin. Or a process server. And if he gives you any grief, I'll threaten to call the health department about the rat problem."

Chris's eyes widen. "You have a rat problem?"

"No." She winks at him. "But the health department doesn't know that."

"Thanks. I owe you one," I tell her as I rush through the final chords of what I've come to think of as our song. Time to go somewhere more private, where I can have Chris all to myself and find out what he flew all the way across the country to get off his chest.

"Just give me a raincheck for Macho Taco. I have a feeling you're going to be otherwise occupied tonight. And you're buying." She glances around the bar, then points to an empty table in the back. "Table six is open. I'll bring you a couple of vodka and sodas."

"Make his an old-fashioned." I stand, putting a possessive hand on Chris's shoulder. Stupid, I know. Denice is my friend. And it's not like Chris is going to be interested in her. At least, I don't think he is. But jealousy is a green-eyed monster, and it's not always rational.

"You got it."

Denice heads for the bar to get our drinks, and Chris and I slide into the dimly lit corner booth she directed us to. I wait until after she's dropped them off to ask the question that's been burning a hole through my brain since I looked up and saw my boyfriend—if that's what he is—leaning against the piano like he's Michelle Pfeiffer in *The Fabulous Baker Boys*.

"What are you doing here?" I realize almost immediately how shitty that sounds. Like my heart didn't skip ten beats when I saw him, which couldn't be further from the truth. "I mean, I'm glad you are. But I thought you had commitments back in San Francisco."

"I did," he says, his tone turning tentative. "But I don't anymore."

Okay, color me confused. I frown at him over the rim of my glass. "What about your job?"

He lifts his own glass and sips. "My job is here. Or, at least, it can be, if I want it to."

I almost drop my drink, barely managing to set it down on the table with a shaking hand. "Are you serious?"

His free hand reaches across the table and snags mine. "As a triple pirouette."

"But you're a principal dancer for one of the best ballet companies in the world. I know how hard you worked to get there. I can't let you give that up." And grow to resent me in a month, a year, or whenever the doubts creep in and he starts to regret the choice he made.

"The way I see it, I'm not giving. I'm gaining." Without releasing my hand, he slides around the table so he's sitting next to me. He's so close. I'm drowning in the fresh, clean scent of his shampoo and the warmth of his fingers in mine. Fuck, I've missed him. So much. I've been walking around like a zombie, except it's not my brain that's been ripped out, it's my heart.

"I didn't tell you this before because I didn't want to get your hopes up if things fell through," he continues, his voice quiet but earnest. "I didn't come to New York two weeks ago just to see you. My agent got me an audition. For a brand-new Broadway show."

"Broadway?"

He nods, excitement dancing in his eyes and softening his strong jaw. "It's a tribute to some of theater's great choreographers. Agnes deMille. Jerome Robbins. Gower Champion. Bob Fosse."

"And you got in?"

"I got in."

A kernel of hope starts to take root in my chest, making it feel hot and tight. "Are you sure that's what you want?"

"Hmm . . . let me think. Stay in San Francisco, all alone. Or move to New York to be on Broadway and with my boyfriend." He lifts my hand to his lips and kisses it. "Seems like a no-brainer to me."

"It's a big leap." What if the show flops? Or he hates the grind of performing eight times a week?

"I'm a dancer. Leaping is my forte." He smiles fades and he bites his lip, suddenly tentative again. "But now it's my turn to ask you. Is this what you want? Us, together, for real? If it's too much, too soon, we can slow down. Manhattan is a big island. We could probably go weeks, if not months, without running into each other."

"Shut up." I know a better way to stop his crazy talk. I take his face between my hands and kiss him, hard and fast, not caring if my bastard of a boss or anyone else is watching. "Of course I want this. I've wanted it since I saw you walking across the quad, looking like you came straight off the pages of an Abercrombie & Fitch catalog. Wanted it more the more I got to know you. I was just waiting for you to want it, too."

"Thank fuck." He lowers his forehead to mine. "Because I don't know what I would have done if you turned me down."

"Like that was going to happen." I go to kiss him again, but my bastard boss picks that inopportune moment to stroll past, giving me the evil eye and tapping his watch. I straighten up and clear my throat.

"I'd better get back to work. This is my last set. Stay and wait for me to finish? I'll have Denice bring you another old-fashioned."

Chris wraps an arm around me, hugging me to his side. "You know I will. But make it a club soda. I want to be totally sober so I'll remember every last second of this night when I wake up with you in the morning."

Damn. He sure knows how to sweet-talk a guy. My boss is out of sight, so I give Chris that kiss, a long, lingering one that speaks of plans and promises. Then I slide out of the booth and stand, turning back to shoot him one last question before I take my place at the piano. "Got any requests?"

He takes a sip of his drink, and I'm momentarily distracted by the way his Adam's apple bobs in the strong column of his throat when he swallows. Christ, that's hot. This set is going to be the fastest one I've ever played. Every song at double—maybe even triple—time.

Then he speaks, snapping me out of my temporary trance. "I was hoping you'd go apartment hunting with me tomorrow."

"Me?" I'm more than willing to tag along, but I'm not sure how much help I'll be.

"Yeah. I could use your input." He knocks back the rest of

his old-fashioned, almost as if he needs some liquid courage for whatever it is he's about to say next. "Your place is great, but I'm, uh, looking for something a little bigger. Like large enough for two people. Maybe with a second bedroom where my boyfriend can put his keyboard. In case someday—when he's ready—he wants to move in."

Not exactly the sort of request I had in mind, but I'll take it. More than take it. There's only one fly in the ointment.

"What about your parents?" I ask. "Won't they get suspicious if we start living together?"

"They know. I came out to them." His chest puffs out a little, and mine does too with pride for my brave ballet boy. "I didn't want to start our relationship with that hanging over our heads. I'm not hiding you. You're too important to me."

I'm almost afraid to ask how they took it, but I don't have to. Chris answers my unspoken question.

"They were surprisingly okay. It helped that my sister was there when I told them. They want to meet you when they come visit."

Wow. We're already at the meet-the-parents stage. I'm grinning like an idiot and my heart's doing a happy little tap dance in my rib cage. "I think I can manage that."

"Good." He shoos me toward the Steinway. "Go. The sooner you start playing, the sooner you finish. And the sooner we can get out of here."

I like the way he thinks. And I've got the perfect song to open the set with. Who cares that it's the last one I played before my break?

I'll just play it again.

-Epilogue-

Chris

"I'm going to take off. See you at the theater."

I glance at my watch. The Omega Speedmaster David gave me on the one-year anniversary of our second first kiss. My call time's not for another hour and a half, and I know the orchestra doesn't have to be there before I am.

"What's wrong? You nervous?" I can't think why he would be. He's subbed Broadway shows before. Okay, so it's his first time subbing for the show I'm in, but he's had the score for weeks and he can play his part blindfolded. I should know. I've heard him practicing for hours on the Yamaha Clavinova acoustic piano in the spare room of our apartment on the Upper West Side. My anniversary gift to him.

"No. I, uh, just have some stuff to do before showtime."

He's shuffling his feet and avoiding eye contact, two sure signs he's hiding something. Whatever it is, I fight my instinct to grill him. Things are good between us. I trust him. He'll tell me what's going on when he's ready.

Won't he?

I shoo away the doubt crows and plant a rough, possessive kiss on his lips. "Okay. See you there."

He gives me a semireassuring smile and leaves, but I can tell he's still distracted, off in his own world. I spend the next hour or so doing my pre-show ritual—stretches, vocal warmups, listening to Ricky Martin on my headphones to get me pumped up—and obsessing about whatever it is David's keeping from me. Then I sling my dance bag over my shoulder and catch a number 3 express train downtown to the theater.

It's only about twenty minutes from my door to the stage door. I say hello to the handful of castmates huddled around the sign-in sheet, scrawl my initials next to my name, and head for my dressing room.

"Hey, Beak."

I grimace at the nickname. It's affectionate when David uses it, a loving reference to my Roman nose, curved like an eagle's beak. But coming from my dance partner and company bestie, Alyssa, it's somewhat less charming. Even though I know she doesn't mean anything by it.

Alyssa's the one who took me under her wing and showed this Broadway virgin the ins and outs of working on the Great White Way. She has more Broadway credits than anyone else in the ensemble. That's why she'd gotten the honor of donning the Legacy Robe on opening night. The robe gets handed down from musical to musical, theater to theater, each show adding a decorative panel before passing it on. It's a tradition for the wearer to circle the stage three times, letting cast members touch it for good luck, then to visit all the dressing rooms to "bless" the production.

I reach out and tweak her ponytail. "I told you. Only David can call me that. One more time and I'll drop you in the middle of our duet in the second act."

"You wouldn't."

She's right. I wouldn't. But it's fun to tease her. Just like she enjoys needling me. "Fine. I won't drop you. I'll just stumble a little when I've got you in the press lift."

She lets that jibe pass without a snappy rejoinder, which isn't like her. Looks like David isn't the only one who's not their usual self today.

"Did my eyes deceive me, or did I just see your fine-ass boyfriend in the green room?"

Speak—or think—of the devil. I swear, I'm half convinced Alyssa's a mind reader. She's more accurate than *The Mentalist*. Or that guy on *Psych*.

A surge of hope—and happiness—rises inside me. Maybe I can talk to him before I go get into costume. Quell the irrational anxiety building in my chest.

I start to head for the stairs that lead to the lounge area where the performers hang out when they're not on stage, but she stops me with a hand on my arm and a shake of her head.

"Not anymore. He went down to the pit about fifteen minutes ago. Said he wanted to get a feel for the keyboard before they opened the house."

"Yeah. He's subbing for Chip tonight."

Even though I'm disappointed I won't be able to catch David before the show starts, I can't stop my chin from lifting with pride. He's worked hard to build a reputation and establish relationships with the Broadway musicians. And it's paying off. I wouldn't be surprised if he's offered a permanent position in a pit orchestra before the year's out. I just hope it's here, with my show. There's nothing I'd like better than having him work with me, dancing for him every night.

"Ooh, it's his first time with us, right?" I nod, and she rubs her hands together. "He must be excited."

I shrug and look down at the tips of my Stan Smiths. "I guess so."

"What do you mean, 'I guess so?'"

"I don't know. He's been acting kind of weird all day."

Alyssa wrinkles her nose, drawing her brows together and creasing her forehead with worry lines. "Like, weird how?"

"Jittery. Evasive." I stuff my hands into my pockets and rock back and forth. "I think he's hiding something from me."

"Like what?"

"If I knew, he wouldn't be hiding it from me."

"Good evening, ladies and gentlemen of the *Dancing Shoes* company," our stage manager's voice booms over the loudspeaker. "This is your half-hour call. Thirty minutes to curtain."

I swear under my breath and hike my bag up higher on my shoulder. "I'd better go get into costume and makeup."

"Okay, but I wouldn't worry too much about David if I were you. I've seen how that boy looks at you. He's totally smitten."

"Smitten? Who uses that word anymore?"

"Me. And the Urban Dictionary. Trust me. It's in there." She turns on her heel and flounces off, blowing me a kiss over her shoulder as she goes. "See you on stage, Beak."

"What did I warn you about calling me that?" I say to her back as she sashays away. "Wait until we get to the lift. You're going down."

But of course she doesn't. The performance goes off without

a hitch, as always. We're professionals, after all. Although I do give in to temptation and manage to sneak a couple of not-so-professional glances at David in the pit, all serious and adorable as he tickles the ivories, his hair flopping over his furrowed brow to the beat of the music. Once we even lock eyes, and an endearingly shy smile flits about the corners of his mouth.

The knot of tension in my stomach eases a little. There, my head says to my heart. *See? Alyssa's right. David's crazy about you. No reason to panic.*

When the show's over and we've bowed our last bow, all I want is to rush offstage, find David, and tell him how proud of him I am. Okay, yeah, and kiss the shit out of him, too. You know what they say. Actions speak louder than words.

But tonight we're collecting for Broadway Cares/Equity Fights Aids, the charity that draws on the talents of the theater community to raise money to help provide essential services for people with HIV/AIDS and other critical illnesses. Which means that I have to stay on stage for a few more minutes and then go into the lobby with my bright red BC/EFA bucket, collecting donations from audience members as they leave the theater.

I try to catch David's eye one more time as Alyssa, our dance captain, takes a handheld mic from the stage manager and begins her please-break-out-your-wallets-for-a-good-cause speech. But he's not behind the keyboard. He's not anywhere in the pit.

The doubt crows start circling again, but I shake them off. There's nothing all that unusual about musicians packing it in as soon as they're done playing. I'm sure David's waiting for me in the green room. I'll catch up with him there.

I turn my attention to Alyssa, who should be wrapping up

her speech about now. Instead, I'm surprised to hear her mention my name.

"Chris, could you come up here?"

Huh? What is she doing? This isn't part of her usual BC/EFA schtick.

I shuffle forward, thinking maybe this is some sort of payback for me threatening to drop her. Then I see a familiar, well-loved face peeking out from the wings, and my heart lodges in my throat, making it difficult to breathe.

"We've got a special surprise for you tonight, Chris," Alyssa continues into the mic so everyone can hear. "For all of you, really."

She gestures to the audience, and a murmur of anticipation ripples through the crowd. "I mean it's not every day you get to witness—well, I'll let David, our fabulous keyboard player this evening, explain everything. Come on out, David."

He enters the stage, gives the audience an awkward wave, and crosses to center, where Alyssa meets him and engulfs him in a bear hug. I could swear he mouths thank you to her, confusing me even more. What is he up to? Why is Alyssa hugging him, and what is he thanking her for? Sure, she's become one of my closest friends during the run of the show, and she and David have gotten to know each other as a result. But I didn't realize they were on a hugs-and-thanks-for-the-favor basis.

Alyssa releases him and I hear her whisper, "You got this," before she hands him the mic and gives him a gentle push in my direction. Up close, I realize for the first time how nervous he is. His smile is shaky, his cheeks pale, and there's a line of sweat at his brow.

"Hey," he says. The quiet greeting is only for me, not the audience, seeing as the mic is down at his side.

"Hey." I smile back, I hope reassuringly.

He raises the mic to his lips. Time seems to stop, and my heart along with it. He's not the only one who's nervous. I'm as jumpy as a chorus girl at her Broadway debut. But it's not because I'm worried about what he's going to say. It's because I think—I hope—I know what's about to happen.

David shuffles his feet. "So, I, uh, suppose you're wondering what we're doing up here."

"You could say that."

The audience, and the cast behind me, titters. David reaches out with his free hand and takes one of mine. "Of all the gin joints, in all the towns, in all the world, you walked into mine a little over a year ago and upended my life. But if I'm honest, you've been doing that since the first time I saw you back at the conservatory. Because that was when I knew you were going to own my heart."

He goes to one knee, and there's an audible, collective gasp from the crowd.

"I loved you then, I love you now, I'll love you always. And that's how long I want us to be together. Always."

He gives some sort of signal to Alyssa, who relays it to the cast behind her. In unison, they raise signs spelling out *Will You Marry Me?*

My brain's buzzing, all the pieces falling into place. So that's what she and David have been up to. And this is what being proposed to feels like. It's a confusing combination of out-of-my-mind overjoyed mixed with a bit of shock/terror. But mostly I feel wanted. Completely, profoundly, beautifully wanted.

He drops my hand. For a moment I'm confused, the loss of physical contact almost painful, until I realize he's pulled a ring out of his pocket. The shiny silver band gleams up at me between his outstretched fingers. "Marry me, Chris, and stay with me forever."

My gaze flits to Alyssa, the cast with their signs, the audience, on the edges of their seats, then finally back to David, who is staring up at me expectantly. "You did all this?"

He nods.

"Why?"

"I thought I made that pretty clear." He holds the ring up a little higher. "I'm proposing."

"I know that. I'm just surprised you'd do it here. In front of all these people. You hate grand romantic gestures. Especially public ones."

"Yeah." His eyes find mine, the heat in them so intense it almost sucks the air out of me. "But you love it."

He's right. I do. "True. But there's something I love more."

"There is?"

"Yeah." My heart's pounding so loud I'm pretty sure they can hear it all the way in the back row of the balcony. "You."

"Does that mean you'll marry me?" he asks, his voice bordering on desperate. "I'm dying down here."

The words won't come, emotion clogging them in my throat, so now it's my turn to nod.

"Is that a yes?" someone from the audience calls out. "Raise the mic. We can't hear you."

David slips the ring on my finger and stands, bringing the mic back to his mouth. When he speaks, it's to the audience, but his eyes don't leave mine. "It's a yes."

"Then kiss him, dammit," someone else yells. The crowd picks it up and starts a chant.

"Kiss him, kiss him, kiss him . . ."

I can't help myself. I need to touch him. I reach out and brush a stray lock of his perpetually disheveled hair off his cheek. "Our public has spoken."

He shrugs and smiles. "Then I guess there's only one thing we can do."

"What's that?"

"Give them what they want."

He hands the microphone to Alyssa, loops an arm around my neck, and pulls me to him. Our lips meet, and everyone around us—cast, crew, audience—erupts in cheers and applause.

Later, at the bar around the corner where the cast likes to congregate after the show, we'll probably swap stories about tonight. Alyssa will say how surprised she'd been when David reached out to her for help, and how hard it had been to keep her mouth shut and not spoil the surprise. David will insist that for a long minute there, he was afraid he'd made a huge mistake and I was going to say no. I'll tell him he was an idiot for thinking I'd ever let him go, then kiss him for all I'm worth to make sure he's convinced.

But for now, the whoops and hollers of the crowd around us fade to black and it's just him and me. The way it always should have been.

The way it always would be.

***

ACKNOWLEDGEMENTS

Thank you for reading Play It Again. I hope you enjoyed it and would consider leaving a review.

If you read the dedication, you'll know that David and Chris are based on my real-life friends and neighbors of this same names. This novella is a fictionalized version of their storybook romance. Yes, I took some liberties, but there's a lot of true stuff in there, too. They really did meet as students at a college conservatory; David is a fabulous pianist (you should see his one-man Liberace show); Chris is a former professional ballet dancer who now teaches dance to kids (and yes, his nickname is Beak); David was out in college and Chris wasn't; and they met again years later, after Chris's divorce, rekindled their relationship, and eventually married. They are truly two of my favorite people in the world, and I can't thank them enough for allowing me to make them secondary characters in The Billionaire In Her Bed and now the heroes of Play It Again.

Thanks also to my fab editor, Jane Haertel, who really helped make this thing shine; to Tessa Bailey and Alexa Riley for giving me the opportunity to write this fun, sexy story for the Read Me Romance podcast; to David Panak for being my beta/sensitivity reader; to my writing tribe, the MTBs, for doing their best at the nearly impossible task of keeping me sane; and, as always, to my ever supportive husband and daughter.

Want a FREE book? Then sign up for my newsletter at:

www.reginakyle.com/subscribe

You'll receive a FREE digital copy of Summer Stock, my sweet-but-sexy second chance romance between a Broadway director and the leading lady he left behind on his road to the Great White Way.

I enjoy interacting with readers, and I'm easy to find on the interwebs. You can follow me on any or all of the following platforms for teasers, giveaways, book bargains, planner tips (yeah, I'm a planner geek), and even the occasional recipe:

Facebook: www.facebook.com/reginakyleauthor
Instagram: www.instagram.com/romancebyregina/
Goodreads: www.goodreads.com/goodreadscomreginakyle
Bookbub: https://www.bookbub.com/profile/regina-kyle

And for more fun stuff, like exclusive excerpts, special giveaways, and first crack at open spots on my ARC review crew, you can join my readers' group, the aptly named Regina's Rabble Rousers, at:

www.facebook.com/groups/351200645062126/.

Come play with us!

I love hearing from readers and would love to hear from you. Until, then, happy reading!

More Books By Regina Kyle

If you liked this book, you may want to try:

Worthington Sisters Series
The Billionaire In Her Bed
A Nanny For The Reclusive Billionaire

The Art Of Seduction Series
Triple Threat
Triple Time
Triple Dare
Triple Score

Harlequin Dare
Dirty Work

Ashland Falls Novellas
Summer Stock
Sugar Plum Seduction